Real-Life CRIMES

... and how they were solved

The Bridgewater Four

Murder at Yew Tree Farm

Bruises: Black and Blue

Rob, Burn and Kill

UK £1.50 Republic of Ireland IR£1.75 Malta M£1.25

Real-Life CRIMES

... and how they were solved

Contents

Volume 6 Part 81

COMING IN PART 82

CRIME CASE STUDY

The Luton Sack Murder: An unidentified woman's body was found in a river. Her killer was eventually brought to justice because of a spelling mistake and a fingerprint on a bottle

THE INVESTIGATORS

Coroner to the Stars: As Chief Medical Examiner of Los Angeles Thomas Noguchi was involved in many famous cases. He conducted post-mortems on Bobby Kennedy and Marilyn Monroe

INCRIMINATING EVIDENCE

The Biting Bandit: A thief was roaming the streets of Homestead, biting his victims before running off with their valuables. In the space of four weeks he attacked 10 men – one three times!

HOW TO MAKE SURE YOUR COLLECTION IS COMPLETE

To be sure of getting your copies each week, either place a regular order with your newsagent or take out a subscription.

HOW TO TAKE OUT A SUBSCRIPTION

(UK and Republic of Ireland only)
We will deliver REAL-LIFE CRIMES at no extra cost. Simply write to REAL-LIFE CRIMES Subscriptions, PO Box 1, Hastings, TN35 4TJ, or telephone 0424 755755.

How to pay
You can pay by cheque, postal order or credit card, and when your subscription is due to expire a renewal letter will be sent to you asking whether you wish to continue your collection.

You may order as many copies as you like, but we suggest a minimum of 10 parts. Please include payment with your order and be sure to state the part number of the first copy you want. You can calculate the amount to pay by multiplying the cover price by the number of parts required, for example 10 issues x £1.50/IR£1.75 will cost £15/IR£17.50 (postage and packing are free).

Cheques or postal orders should be made payable to Woodgate (Eaglemoss) Ltd.

If paying by credit card, be sure to state the cardholder's name, the type of card (e.g. Access or Visa), the card number and the expiry date.

BINDERS

UK and Republic of Ireland: Binders are priced at £5.95/IR£5.95. To get your binder, send a cheque or postal order, made payable to Woodgate (Eaglemoss) Ltd, to REAL-LIFE CRIMES Binders, PO Box 1, Hastings, TN35 4TJ. For payment by credit card, telephone 0424 755755.
Australia: Binders are priced at $14.95. To get your binder, send a cheque or money order, made payable to Bissett Magazine Services Pty Ltd, to REAL-LIFE CRIMES Binders, PO Box 315, Vermont, Victoria, or telephone (03) 872 4000.

ACKNOWLEDGEMENTS

Authors: Patrick Pender
Brian Innes
Ray Granger
Photography: David Hendley
For their valuable help and advice, our thanks to:
Emeritus Professor Alan Usher

Picture acknowledgements
Front cover: Syndication International. **1769:** Syndication International/News Team International Ltd. **1770:** Solo Syndication/Solo Syndication/John Frost Newspapers. **1771:** Solo Syndication. **1772:** Solo Syndication/John Frost Newspapers. **1773:** Press Association/Solo Syndication. **1774:** Syndication International/Express Newspapers. **1775:** Solo Syndication/Express Newspapers. **1776:** Express Newspapers/News Team International Ltd. **1777:** Solo Syndication. **1778:** John Frost Newspapers. **1779:** Press Association/Press Association. **1780:** Syndication International/News Team International Ltd. **1781:** John Frost Newspapers/Topham Picture Source. **1782:** University of Sheffield. **1783:** University of Sheffield. **1784:** University of Sheffield. **1785:** Richard Whittington Egan (all). **1786:** UPI Bettmann/The Kansas Historical Society. **1787:** Minnesota Historical Society/Glasgow Herald & Evening Times. **1790:** Bruce Coleman Ltd/Minnesota Historical Society.

Published by:
Eaglemoss Publications Ltd
7 Cromwell Road
London SW7 2HR
Circulation Manager:
Gary Neale
Subscription and Back Numbers Enquiries:
Customer Services 0424 755755

Editorial offices:
REAL-LIFE CRIMES
Midsummer Books Ltd
179 Dalling Road
London W6 0ES

Managing Editor: Stan Morse
Editors: Chris Bishop
Trisha Palmer
Production Editor: Sheryl Fellows
Design: Vanessa Stoddart
Picture Researchers: Veneta Bullen
Davina Bullen
Sophie Mortimer

Colour reproduction:
Chroma Graphics Pte Ltd, Singapore
Printed in Great Britain by: Varnicoat Ltd

The boy was nearing the end of his paper round when he wheeled his bicycle into the yard of Yew Tree Farm. But it was a round he was never to finish. A close-range shotgun blast took care of that.

MURDER AT YEW TREE FARM

Thirteen-year-old Carl Bridgewater lived about a mile from Yew Tree Farm, in the small town of Wordsley. It was a comfortable, rural area, situated just to the west of the urban sprawl of the West Midlands. Carl had only just started a regular paper round with Davies' newsagent, and the farm was his third last delivery.

WHO KILLED CARL BRIDGEWATER?

It was a warm late-summer afternoon as Carl Bridgewater cycled down the hill from Wordsley, along Lawnswood Road and towards Yew Tree Farm. In the Staffordshire town many people were out enjoying the last of the summer sunshine, and several of them waved at 13-year-old Carl as he pedalled around the town on his after-school newspaper round. It was Tuesday 19 September 1978.

Carl had taken up the round with Mr Davies, a local newsagent, a few weeks before, and enjoyed cycling around the area. Now as Carl approached the farm he was almost finished. He had just three more papers to deliver before he could set off home.

At nearby Wordsley Hospital Dr Angus

Macdonald had finished his duties for the day and left to drive home. His route took him along Lawnswood Road, the way Carl had cycled less than an hour before.

Doctor calls at farm

Many of Dr Macdonald's patients were elderly and he liked to keep an eye on their welfare. At the bottom of Lawnswood Road lived retired farmer Fred Jones and his cousin Mary Poole; they were both well into their 70s and suffered from arthritis. On impulse, Dr Macdonald decided to pay them a visit. He slowed his car down and turned left into the drive that led to the rear of their home, Yew Tree Farm.

Mr Jones, a widower, had given up farming a few years before. The fields surrounding the house had been sold to a neighbour, Hubert Wilkes, who farmed the adjacent Holloway House Farm.

There were no cars in the farmyard and the doctor guessed his patients must be out, but he decided to knock anyway. But as he approached the door he sensed something was wrong. The door was ajar, and on the jamb and around the lock the paint and wood had been chipped and damaged. Someone had obviously forced it with the edge of a garden spade, which was now propped against the wall.

Dr Macdonald hesitated then, concerned for his elderly patients, stepped inside. The house was chaos: drawers had been tipped out, and crockery and ornaments were smashed and scattered over the floor. As he went through to the living room the doctor noticed a young boy lying

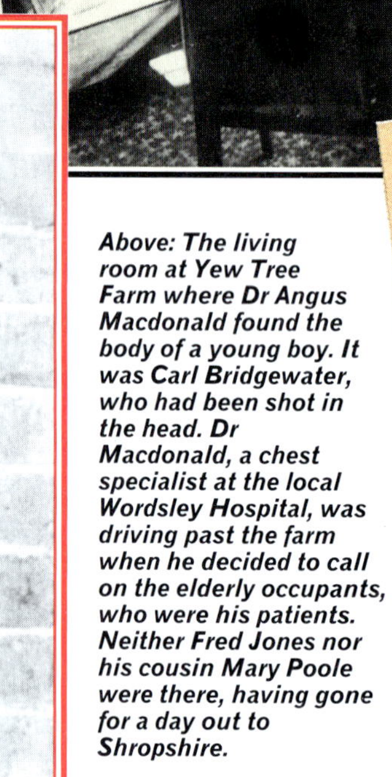

Above: The living room at Yew Tree Farm where Dr Angus Macdonald found the body of a young boy. It was Carl Bridgewater, who had been shot in the head. Dr Macdonald, a chest specialist at the local Wordsley Hospital, was driving past the farm when he decided to call on the elderly occupants, who were his patients. Neither Fred Jones nor his cousin Mary Poole were there, having gone for a day out to Shropshire.

Left: A scene of crime officer from the Staffordshire police brushes the doorway of Yew Tree Farm for fingerprints. The paintwork and the wood around the lock had been damaged; clearly the killers had forced the door open. Some antiques were missing from the house, and police concluded that Carl had probably stumbled on a gang of armed burglars and had been shot by them.

Daily

THURSDAY, SEPTEM

Carl was 13. On his paper
news boy' came face to
gang of burglars. They s

IN CO
BLO

By AUBREY CHALMERS

THE MEN with the shotgun did not care about Carl Bridgewater. They did not care that he was only 13 years old.

They did not care that he was doing well at school, was a patrol leader at Scouts.

They did not care that Carl had come into the house on his newspaper delivery round only as a kindness to the frail, old couple who lived there—to leave their paper on a chair so they would not have to go outside and bend down to pick it up.

The men with the shotgun did not care. What they did care about was not being identified as the gang of burglars he had disturbed. One of them pulled the trigger and shot Carl in the head at pointblank range. 'It was a coldblooded killing and callous in the extreme,' the policeman who is hunting for the boy's murderers said yesterday.

Detective Chief Superintendent Bob Stewart, head of Staffordshire CID, believes Carl may even have recognised one of the gang.

Silenced

Carl, from Ascot Gardens, Wordsley, near Stourbridge, West Midlands, had been a paper boy for two
months. He earned about £3 a week for doing a 1½ mile
run of 24 houses on his bicycle, delivering the evening
paper. When he got to Yew Tree Farm, near Wombourne,
he always opened the back door and left the paper on a
chair for 79-year-old Miss Mary Poole and her cousin
Fred Jones, 76.

On Tuesday, unknown to Carl, they were out fo
the day. He found that the door opened as usual—it ha
been forced. He left the paper on the chair, turned to g
and, said Mr Stewart, 'I am sure that he disturbed th
burglars. He had done his job and was presumably o
his way. Why did they go to the trouble of taking hi
into the house and shooting him? It is possible that t
lad recognised one of them and had to be silenced.'

Carl, in a blue anorak, set off at 3.50 p.m. Yew T
Farm, on the corner of the A449 Wolverhampton
Kidderminster road and Lawnswood Road, was his t
last call. Next stop was to be Mrs Katherine Wood,
lives nearby. She saw Carl about 4.15 passing her d

Turn to Page 2, Col 1

INSIDE: Fe... Prize Crossword 22

Right: Detective Chief Superintendent Robert Stewart, leading the murder enquiry, examines some of the Victorian antiques dropped by the robbers as they fled from the scene. They got away with a few small items – warming pans, fire irons and a carving set – that were worth about £500. Nevertheless, police released and publicised details of the stolen pieces in the hope that they would turn up in an antique shop.

Mail

WHEN YOUR CHILD GOES MISSING SEE PAGE 12

8p (CHANNEL ISLANDS 9p)

d the kindly e with a him dead.

rl Bridgewater, newspaper boy—and murder victim

Left: The callous murder of an innocent young boy shocked the country. The killers, if found, could expect no mercy. And public pressure on the police called for them to find the culprits as soon as possible.

on the settee, apparently asleep. The doctor stepped closer and gasped: the boy's head was smothered in blood. It was the paperboy Carl Bridgewater. He had been cold-bloodedly murdered.

Dr Macdonald knew it was important not to touch anything, and so telephoned the police from a neighbouring cottage. When they arrived he returned to the farm with them, and pronounced Carl dead. The boy was slumped on his side with his feet on the floor. It looked as if he might have been sitting down when he died. He had been shot in the left side of the head from very close range with a shotgun.

Shortly afterwards, Fred Jones and Mary Poole arrived home. They had been for a drive out into the Shropshire hills. They were horrified, and had no idea who could have committed such a dreadful crime.

Scene of crime examination

Detectives worked long into the night examining the scene. A window pane at the front of the house had been smashed, and there was glass scattered on the carpet. In the gardens and grounds they found various antiques from the house, hidden in long grass and bushes. The house had been thoroughly searched and ransacked.

It was clear that Carl had disturbed the robbers. He had already delivered his paper when he was waylaid; that day's copy of the *Wolverhampton Express and Star* was in the box by the door where he always left it. Carl's canvas delivery bag with the two remaining papers in it was still slung around his lifeless body. Police found his yellow bike, which he normally left outside the house, in an old disused pig sty.

Cold-bloodedly killed

Detective Chief Superintendent Robert Stewart, head of Staffordshire CID, and his colleagues all agreed that Carl had probably innocently walked in on a crime in progress. It looked as if he had been marched inside, ordered to sit on the settee and then shot in cold blood.

Stewart and the rest of his team were shocked and baffled by what seemed to be an inexplicable killing. They knew that even the most ruthless of criminals would normally never harm a child – it was part of the criminal code. In Stewart's experience people who victimised children were reviled by other criminals to the point of having to be segregated from them for their own safety in jail.

For a robber to gun down a boy like this was unheard of. There seemed to be only two possibilities. The killer was either a psychopath, perhaps fired up on drugs, or Carl had stumbled upon someone he knew, someone who could not afford to have the paperboy identify him.

The murder of the innocent schoolboy caused outrage throughout the Midlands. The police operation followed two parallel courses. While one group of officers concentrated on the reports of witnesses who claimed to have seen vehicles and people near Yew Tree Farm on the day Carl died, others questioned their informants and combed criminal intelligence files. Yew Tree Farm had contained many valuable antiques, and about £500-worth had been taken. The detectives wanted any information about people selling stolen antiques. They also looked at the records, descriptions and *modus operandi* of hundreds of Midlands-based burglars and robbers.

Witnesses come forward

The house-to-house questioning and appeals in the newspapers and on TV were proving useful. Villains who would normally never speak to the police offered information about people they suspected. Several witnesses reported seeing vehicles parked near the farm between 4 and 4.30 p.m. – the time of Carl's death. The descriptions of the vehicles varied from a blue Ford Cortina estate car to a blue Ford Transit-type van.

At least one witness had seen men walking near the farm at the time of the crime. Another had spotted two men on the road near the farm with a shotgun. These were important pieces of information. The person or people concerned – police had no way of knowing if it was one man or a group of men – must have had a vehicle. The witnesses were pressed hard to remember all they could.

The public was eager to help. A squad of 50 officers based at a murder incident HQ at Wombourne police station was deluged with possible leads and tip-offs, most of them too vague to be of any real use. The detectives were struggling for the vital lead they were hoping for. Then on Friday 30 November they thought they had it.

Detective Chief Superintendent Robert Stewart checks the latest piece of information received at the incident room set up by the Staffordshire police. Christmas was approaching, but at last they looked like they had a break. An elderly couple at a farm only 20 miles away from Yew Tree Farm had been held up by armed robbers and their home ransacked. Investigators felt sure that the two crimes were linked.

THE SUN, Thursday, September 28, 1978

BITTERNESS AND SORROW ON THE MURDERED NEWSBOY'S LAST JOURNEY

THE VILLAGE WEEPS FOR CARL

The death of a child is always tragic, but the execution-style killing of a 13-year-old boy just because he apparently witnessed a robbery was especially horrifying. The outraged villagers of Wordsley attended Carl's funeral, demanding that the police find his killers.

Another farm is raided

That evening the elderly occupants of Chapel Farm in the village of Romsley, near Halesowen, were terrorised by three masked men who burst into their home, armed with a sawn-off shotgun.

Eighty-three-year-old Jack Smith and his three sisters, Mildred, Kathleen and Henrietta, tried to fight off the intruders, but two of the old ladies were hit with the butt of a gun, causing injuries that required hospital treatment. Eventually the bandits got the upper hand, grabbed £300 in cash and fled. But as they tore through the village their beige Austin 1100 car was spotted by a neighbour, who took down the registration number.

The car belonged to a woman living in Birmingham – Linda Galvin. Police files showed she lived with a known criminal, Vincent Hickey. The Romsley robbery was only 20 miles from Yew Tree Farm, and police wondered if the incidents could be linked. Three men armed with a shotgun had attacked an isolated farm occupied by old people. It looked like a similar MO. There had to be a strong chance that it was the same men who had killed Carl.

Detectives tried to arrest 25-year-old Vincent Hickey at Linda Galvin's home in Northfields, Birmingham, on 1 December 1978. Hickey was in bed, but as police knocked at the front door he fled through a rear window and escaped across some fields.

But four days later Hickey went with a solicitor to the police at Bromsgrove, Worcestershire, who were investigating the Romsley hold-up, and gave himself up.

Vincent Hickey had been in regular trouble with the law since his teens. In October he had gone voluntarily to the murder incident room to speak to detectives. They wanted to talk to him because he owned a blue Ford Cortina estate car, and some witnesses had said they had seen this type of vehicle at Yew Tree Farm on the afternoon the paperboy was killed.

Hickey had told the detectives that the car had been scrapped earlier in the year, and he had been allowed to leave the police station without further action. But now he

Left: *The Wordsley newsagent for whom Carl worked displays a police reward poster. Carl's savage murder shocked the local community, and every step was taken to enlist the public in the search for his killers.*

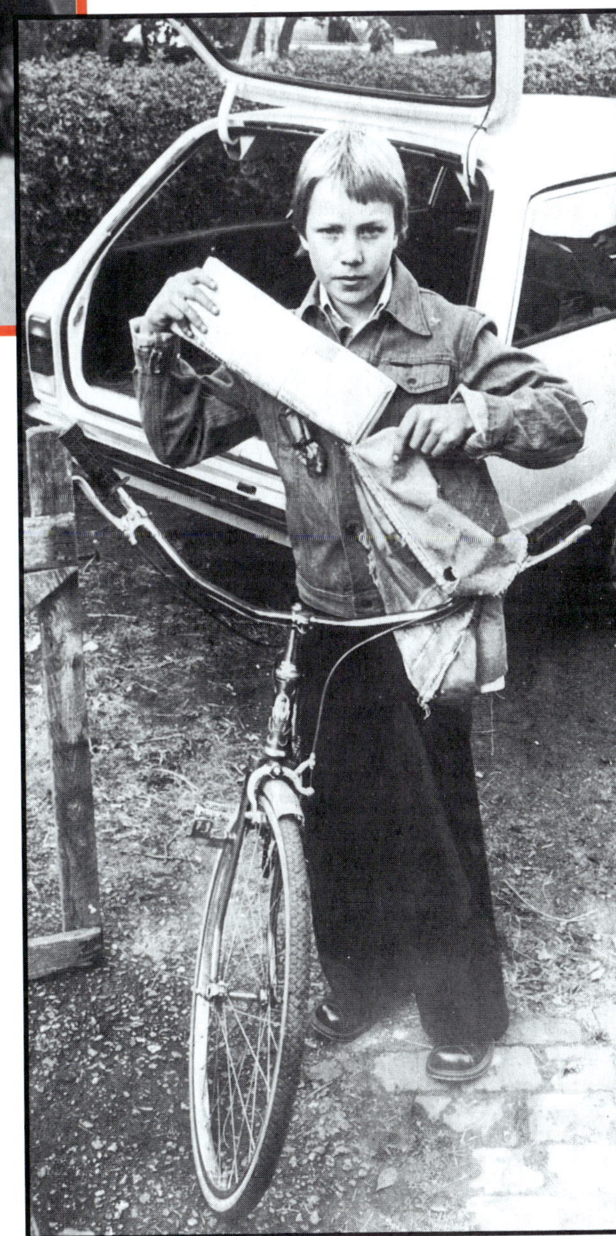

Right: *Two weeks after the killing, Martin Flavell, one of Carl's school friends, helped police to reconstruct the murdered boy's last journey. This reconstruction, together with extensive questioning of local motorists and the widely publicised poster campaign, produced results. A neighbour reported seeing a blue estate car parked at the back of the farmhouse on the afternoon of the murder, and at least a dozen other people confirmed this. One witness was sure that the vehicle was a blue Vauxhall Viva, and that the man driving it was wearing some kind of uniform. But in spite of this lead the police were no nearer solving the case.*

Suspect arrested

Vincent Hickey, questioned about the hold-up at Chapel Farm, was well known to police. In 1977 he had been working with three cousins doing roof repairs. At Rickmansworth, in Hertfordshire, they conned an old man out of £130, then two of them later returned to rob him of about £1,000.

The police quickly caught up with Vincent Hickey, and he volunteered to 'shop' his accomplices in return for a 'deal'. After giving detectives the names, he was charged only with the deception matter and not the subsequent robbery. As a result, he had only been sentenced to a two-year suspended sentence when he appeared for trial in November 1978.

Armed robbery

Earlier in November he had been suspected of being involved in an armed hold-up at a Tesco store at Castle Vale, Birmingham. But the actual robbers were his cousin, 17-year-old Michael Hickey, and two other small-time Birmingham villains, Jimmy Robinson and John Burkett.

Held at gunpoint

They had held several terrified shoppers at gunpoint while they grabbed a bag of money. A shot had been fired into the air by Burkett when the manager tried to chase them. The take had turned out to be disappointing: just a few hundred pounds. They needed to keep on working.

Some months before the Chapel Farm robbery had occured, Vincent and a friend had been to the farm and conned the owner out of £350. He had seen the old man take the cash out of a tin. Vincent and his gang had decided to go back for the rest of the cash.

was in very serious trouble. Not only was he clearly involved in the Romsley case, but detectives candidly told him he was now a hot suspect for the murder of Carl Bridgewater.

But Vincent Hickey was not going to readily confess to anything. A conviction for the Chapel Farm hold-up, involving violence against old people, would mean a long jail sentence. He decided to try for concessions. At first Hickey denied he had been involved in the Chapel Farm robbery and claimed he had only lent the gang the getaway car. But later he offered to name the men who he said had been there.

The detectives encouraged him to talk. Hickey let slip that one of the Romsley robbers was his cousin, 17-year-old Michael Hickey. He wanted to keep the detectives interested, and, tantalisingly, he told them: "Michael knows who killed Carl Bridgewater." The police gave no hint of their reaction, but behind the scenes it had created a great stir.

Experienced officers had a strong hunch that Vincent Hickey might have been at Yew Tree Farm. They thought he was trying to pave the way to inform on others in exchange for special treatment in return. They decided to turn the heat on him a little. The next day he was charged with the Chapel Farm robbery, and then returned to his cell with no further contact.

Hickey was agitated, and asked to see the detectives again. He said he knew who had shot Carl. It was the gunman from the Romsley job, Jimmy Robinson. He offered

Right: Vincent Hickey, an itinerant roofer sidelining in robbery, was involved in looting another farm two months after Carl's murder. Hickey immediately came into the frame for the earlier crime.

Jimmy Robinson was an habitual criminal who had accompanied Vincent Hickey on the robbery at Chapel Farm. Robinson owned a shotgun, which he had used in several robberies, and which made him the prime suspect in the Carl Bridgewater murder.

to take the police to where Robinson and his cousin Michael were living.

Detective Chief Superintendent Stewart and his deputy Detective Chief Inspector Weslea Watson arrived at Bromsgrove to interview Vincent Hickey. After further discussions he said the third man present when Carl was killed was another petty crook, Pat Molloy.

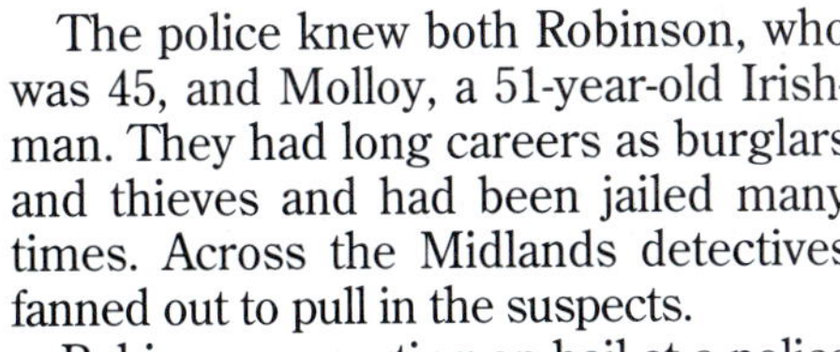

The police knew both Robinson, who was 45, and Molloy, a 51-year-old Irishman. They had long careers as burglars and thieves and had been jailed many times. Across the Midlands detectives fanned out to pull in the suspects.

Robinson, reporting on bail at a police station in connection with another matter, was arrested and taken to Bromsgrove.

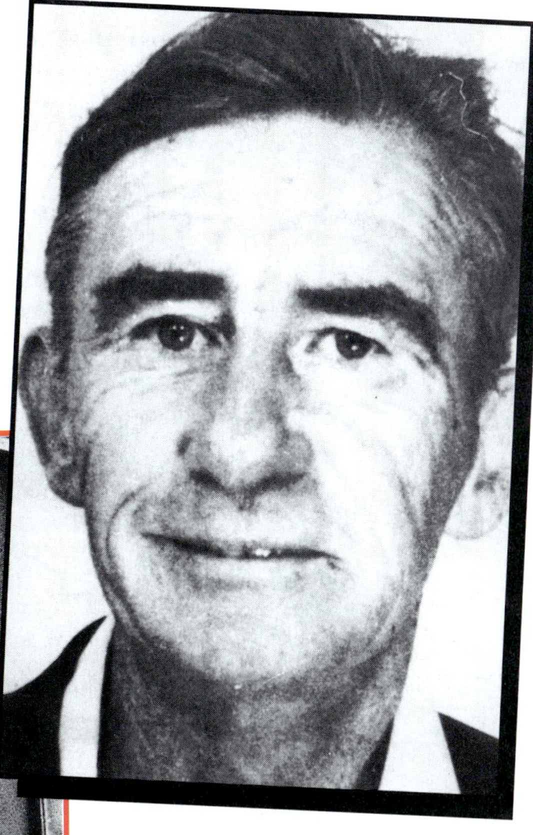

***Right:** Irish-born Pat Molloy was a long-time associate of Jimmy Robinson. Molloy was named by Vincent Hickey as having been involved in the Chapel Farm robbery. After three days of questioning Molloy eventually confessed to having been at Yew Tree Farm when Carl was killed.*

***Below:** The fourth man picked up by the police was Vincent Hickey's cousin, Michael. Although only 17, Michael Hickey was an experienced criminal, who only weeks before had accompanied Jimmy Robinson in the armed robbery of a Tesco store.*

Officers looking for a criminal in connection with a hold-up on a Tesco's store raided his house in Birmingham early in the morning and came up with an unexpected bonus. It was Pat Molloy, who had stayed overnight at his friend's house. They were both arrested.

Over the next few hours complex stories involving several crimes were told. Robinson admitted robbing Chapel Farm and volunteered to take detectives to where he had hidden the gun. But he denied having anything to do with the murder of Carl: he told detectives he couldn't have been at Yew Tree Farm on the fateful day because he was busy planning another job.

Meat robbery alibi

That same night, 19 September, he had broken into a butcher's freezer in Birmingham, stolen a load of meat and sold it in the market the next morning. He had then gone drinking with Molloy and on the following night, 20 September, they had stolen a car and robbed another meat store, this time in Tamworth. On their way back they had been chased by police. Molloy had run off and escaped, but Robinson had been arrested. He had been given a suspended prison sentence.

The detectives listened with interest. They believed Robinson's story about the Birmingham meat raid, but that had happened many hours after the murder of Carl. A crook like Robinson could easily have been on that job too.

By this time Vincent Hickey had been moved to Redditch police station. There he once again indicated he had knowledge of the Yew Tree Farm murder and continued to ask for the Romsley case against him to be dropped. Interviewing detectives became more convinced that Hickey had been at Yew Tree Farm and he was questioned about it over and over again. The detectives needed confessions or someone to inform on the others. None of the suspects' fingerprints had been found at the farm, and there had been a disappointing lack of forensic evidence. None of the eyewitnesses could name anyone they had seen.

Suspect holds his silence

Then, on the afternoon of 8 December, Vincent Hickey told detectives he had been at Yew Tree Farm, but only as a getaway driver. The detectives thought they were on the verge of a big breakthrough, but Hickey refused to say anything further.

After another two days of questioning Hickey again changed his story, saying he had *not* been at Yew Tree Farm. He claimed that the reason he said he was there was a tactic. He was pushing things to the limit, hoping to get a deal on the Romsley case. The detectives thought they were back at square one when some exciting news arrived from Wombourne police station.

Pat Molloy had also been undergoing hours of questioning, and had eventually admitted being at Yew Tree Farm. He said his fellow robbers were Robinson and Michael and Vincent Hickey. He told detectives that he was at the farm when Carl was shot, but he was upstairs at the time. He explained: "I was told it was Jimmy that did it and that it was an accident." Molloy had signed a formal written statement.

Michael Hickey, who had just turned 17, heard through the grapevine that his cousin, Robinson and Molloy had all been arrested. He vanished from the Birmingham area, and went to stay first with relatives in Norfolk and later in Peterborough. He was finally arrested on 20 December. Michael Hickey vehemently denied all knowledge of the Yew Tree Farm incident.

Pat Molloy, who was in custody but still not charged, then changed his original story. Speaking to Detective Chief Inspec-

tor Weslea Watson, Molloy told him that it was Michael who had been holding the gun, not Jimmy Robinson. When this inconsistency was pointed out to him, Molloy said: "I don't know which is correct, it could be either." He said he had a lot to drink before going on the raid, and described his recollection of the events as "hazy". He was charged with the murder of Carl Bridgewater on 28 December.

On 7 January Vincent Hickey was charged. A month later, on 7 February, after consultation with lawyers for the Crown, Michael Hickey and Jimmy Robinson were charged with the same offence.

The Carl Bridgewater trial opened at Stafford Crown Court on 8 October 1979 before Mr Justice Drake. It began with two days of legal argument, at the end of which the judge ruled that no reference could be made to the Chapel Farm robbery which led to the arrests because it would be prejudicial to the interests of the accused.

On trial for murder

The jury was sworn in and the main trial began on 10 October with all four of the accused pleading not guilty. The prosecution opened with the testimony of eight witnesses who had seen a blue car, seven of whom said it was an estate, parked close to Yew Tree Farm at around the time Carl died. Several had described people seen either inside or outside the vehicle. Further, one of them, Mr Mario Sabetta, said he had seen two men, one carrying what appeared to be a shotgun, crossing Lawnswood Road towards the farm from a blue estate car.

Below: A key piece of evidence was that Jimmy Robinson owned a single-barrelled sawn-off shotgun, which he had bought from a local Birmingham gangster. The police made a great deal of the fact that it fired the same type of Eley shell as the gun that had killed Carl. Unfortunately, so did a million other shotguns in the British Isles.

Above: Carl's parents, Brian and Janet Bridgewater, attend the hearing remanding the four armed robbers on charges of murdering their son. Amongst all the controversy since the trial, it is easy to forget they are the people most affected by the vicious crime.

Right: Vincent and Michael Hickey were regulars in the Dog and Partridge pub in Selly Oak, about 10 miles from the murder scene. They claimed to have been celebrating the birth of a friend's child there at the time of the murder. Many of the regulars attested to that fact – but a barmaid also reported an incriminating conversation between Robinson and Molloy.

Evidence

Molloy's confession

Pat Molloy's interviews with Detective Constables John Perkins and Graham Leeke started with him denying all knowledge of the Carl Bridgewater shooting. The interrogation went on through the night of 9 December into the early hours of Sunday 10 December, with Molloy steadfastly pleading his innocence.

Several other detectives were brought in to question him. Then, halfway through Sunday, Molloy asked to see Detective Constable John Perkins alone. He told him: "I was at the farm when the lad got shot, but I didn't know about the gun until after. I was upstairs when it happened. I didn't see it." He went on: "I was told that it was Jimmy that did it and that it was an accident."

Confession through terror

Perkins was then joined by his colleague Detective Constable Leeke. Molloy explained why he had been reluctant to confess. He told the detectives: "I am terrified of the others; they have threatened me with personal injury." Leeke asked him who "the others" were. Molloy responded: "Vinny Hickey and his relation Mickey, and Jimmy Robinson."

Molloy described how the four had gone to the farm in two vehicles, a blue Cortina estate and a borrowed van. He said he was upstairs searching through a chest of drawers when the shooting happened. He told the detectives: "While I was upstairs I heard someone downstairs saying to be careful because there was someone coming.

"I heard a bang"

"I hid for a while and after a while I heard a bang from downstairs. I knew it was a gun being fired. I went downstairs and the three of them were still in the room. They all looked shocked and were shouting at each other. I heard Jimmy say 'it went off by accident'. On the settee I saw the body of the boy. He had been shot in the head. I was appalled and I just ran from the house.

"Since the job I have been threatened by Vinny and Jimmy. I was told I must not admit anything to do with this job, but to turn others in and the police would be satisfied. I can't state my sorrow sufficiently about the murder of that boy."

Molloy dictated a four-page statement, and at 5.30 p.m. on Sunday 10 December he signed it.

Robinson and Molloy had agreed to go on identity parades before eight witnesses, but neither of them had been picked out. Vincent and Michael Hickey had refused to take part in an ID line-up.

Anwar Mohammad, known to Birmingham villains as 'Spider', testified that three weeks before the murder he had sold Jimmy Robinson a single-barrelled shotgun, which Robinson had later shortened by sawing off the barrel. The gun, exhibit 25, was said by the prosecution to have been the one used to kill Carl.

Hidden gun and cartridges

Robinson, who had led police to the gun and 11 cartridges he had hidden on wasteground in Birmingham, admitted it was the one used in the Chapel Farm robbery, but still vigorously denied he had been at Yew Tree Farm. There was no forensic evidence to prove that the weapon was the gun that had killed Carl. A shotgun leaves no telltale identifying marks on the shot it fires, unlike a pistol or rifle. The shot in the cartridge that killed the paperboy was size 5; the shot in the cartridges found with Robinson's gun was size 3.

All the accused had insisted when ques-

tioned that none of them were familiar with the town of Wordsley and the area around Yew Tree Farm. But the prosecution produced a witness who testified that at least two of the defendants had lied. Reg Hickey, a relation of the two cousins, said that he had carried out a number of roofing jobs with Michael and Vincent in Wordsley and the neighbouring areas of Sedgley and Kingswinsford.

Several people testified against the accused, claiming they had had conversations with or overheard parts of conversations between the four in which the job was discussed. Helen Johnston, a barmaid at the Dog and Partridge, a pub frequently used by the four, told the court she had heard a conversation between Molloy and Robinson. Molloy told his friend: "If we are caught and seen by the police you must say the gun went off accidentally."

Several other people, including three prisoners and a prison officer, who had been in the same remand jail as Robinson and the Hickeys before the trial, gave evidence that they had either admitted to the murder or had made partial admissions to them.

In their defence, Robinson and both Hickeys could produce witnesses who gave alibi evidence that they were elsewhere when the shooting took place.

Confession convinces jury

But the prosecution evidence that did the most damage was the statement by Pat Molloy. Under British law it is a strict rule that no person can testify against another facing the same charge unless he is prepared to go into the witness box and answer questions under oath. Thus, in itself Molloy's statement was not evidence against the others.

Molloy refused to go into the witness box on advice from his legal representa-

Campaign

The campaign to free the four began in earnest in 1980 when Michael Hickey's mother, Ann Whelan, contacted the campaigning journalist Paul Foot, then a columnist at the *Daily Mirror*. She claimed that her son and his friends had been convicted of a crime they had not committed.

Foot, who regularly received mail from families who claimed their loved ones were 'innocent' of the crimes for which they had been jailed, was at first sceptical. But as he looked deeper into the affair, the more convinced he became that there had been a miscarriage of justice.

Book published

For the past 13 years Paul Foot has challenged the evidence on which the four were convicted and campaigned for their release. In his book *Murder at the Farm – Who Killed Carl Bridgewater?* Foot has painstakingly examined the evidence and the witnesses whose testimony convicted them.

Foot maintains that Molloy, a man of limited intellect, confessed to a crime he had not committed in order to bring to an end hours of relentless questioning by the police.

He also says that, in his view, the witnesses who saw cars at or near Yew Tree Farm on the day of the murder were well-meaning but inconsistent and vague, and that many other witnesses who gave evidence against the four either had a grudge to settle or were already proven liars.

Foot said: "It was at the very best a threadbare case, unsupported by

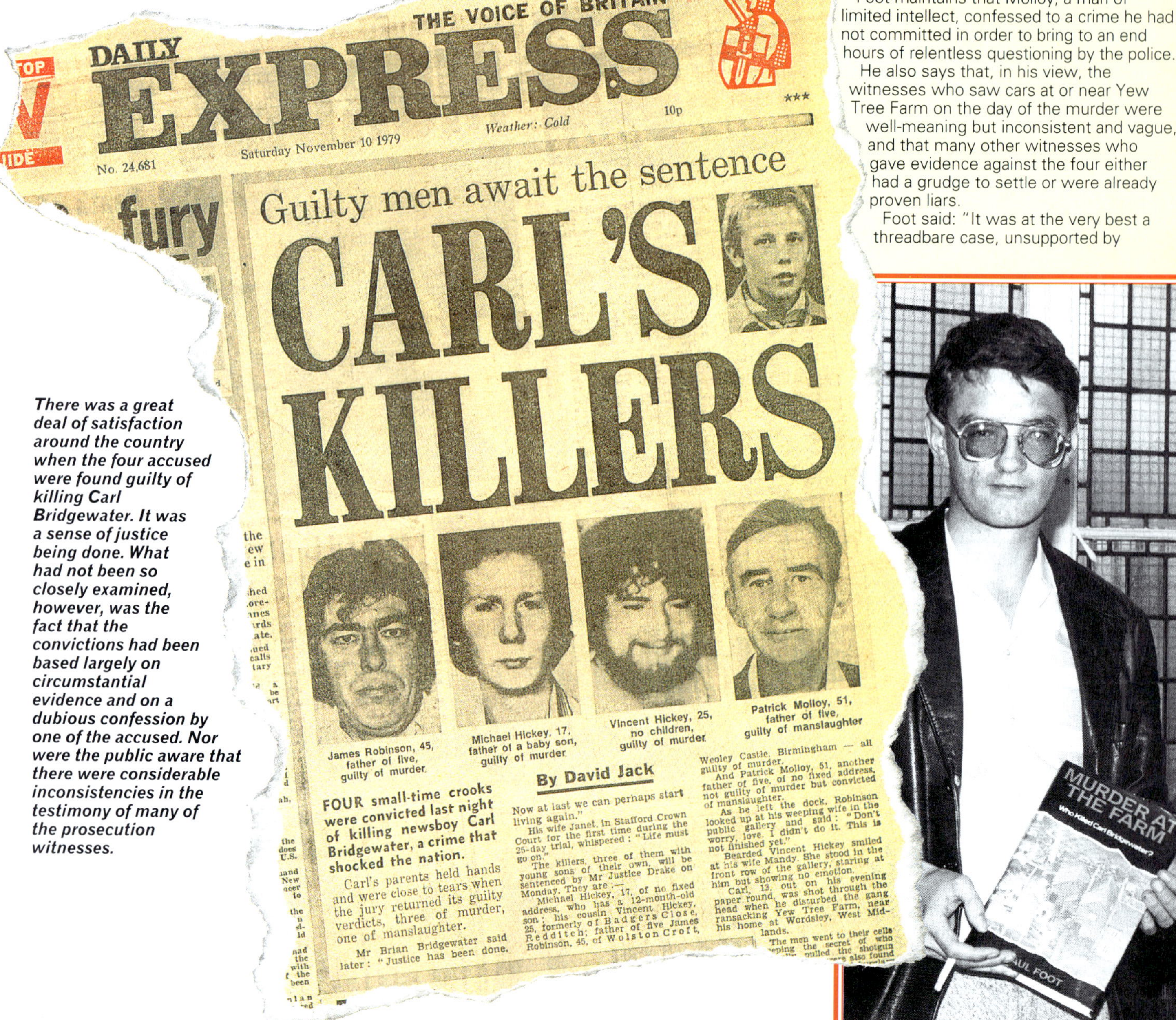

THE VOICE OF BRITAIN

DAILY EXPRESS

No. 24,681 Saturday November 10 1979 Weather: Cold 10p

Guilty men await the sentence

CARL'S KILLERS

James Robinson, 45, father of five, guilty of murder

Michael Hickey, 17, father of a baby son, guilty of murder

Vincent Hickey, 25, no children, guilty of murder

Patrick Molloy, 51, father of five, guilty of manslaughter

By David Jack

FOUR small-time crooks were convicted last night of killing newsboy Carl Bridgewater, a crime that shocked the nation.

Carl's parents held hands and were close to tears when the jury returned its guilty verdicts, three of murder, one of manslaughter.

Mr Brian Bridgewater said later: "Justice has been done. Now at last we can perhaps start living again."

His wife Janet, in Stafford Crown Court for the first time during the 25-day trial, whispered: "Life must go on."

The killers, three of them with young sons of their own, will be sentenced by Mr Justice Drake on Monday. They are:—

Michael Hickey, 17, of no fixed address, who has a 12-month-old son; his cousin Vincent Hickey, 25, formerly of Badgers Close, Redditch; father of five James Robinson, 45, of Wolston Croft, Weoley Castle, Birmingham — all guilty of murder.

And Patrick Molloy, 51, another father of five, of no fixed address, not guilty of murder but convicted of manslaughter.

As he left the dock, Robinson looked up at his weeping wife in the public gallery and said: "Don't worry, love. I didn't do it. This is not finished yet."

Bearded Vincent Hickey smiled at his wife Mandy. She stood in the front row of the gallery, staring at him but showing no emotion.

Carl, 13, out on his evening paper round, was shot through the head when he disturbed the gang ransacking Yew Tree Farm, near his home at Wordsley, West Midlands.

The men went to their cells ...

There was a great deal of satisfaction around the country when the four accused were found guilty of killing Carl Bridgewater. It was a sense of justice being done. What had not been so closely examined, however, was the fact that the convictions had been based largely on circumstantial evidence and on a dubious confession by one of the accused. Nor were the public aware that there were considerable inconsistencies in the testimony of many of the prosecution witnesses.

to free them

The Bridgewater Four have continued to protest their innocence. Jimmy Robinson is seen here making a rooftop protest at Gartree Prison in 1993. Vincent and Michael Hickey have also protested on prison roofs: Michael Hickey spent 89 days on the roof of Long Lartin jail over the winter of 1983/84, by far the longest rooftop protest in British prison history.

forensic evidence..."

But, perhaps even more importantly, Foot makes out a powerful case that Carl Bridgewater was killed by someone completely different, a man who was to commit another murder in an astonishing sequel.

Below: Ann Whelan, Michael Hickey's mother, has never stopped fighting for her son's release. She also persuaded campaigning journalist Paul Foot to take up the cause. Foot's book **Murder at the Farm** *was published in 1986, and once more propelled the case into the limelight.*

tives, and the only hard evidence against him was his own confession. If he gave evidence and retracted it, there was a danger the jury might think he was lying and convict him of murder. If he did not deny making it there was a strong chance that he would not be convicted of murder but of the much lesser charge of manslaughter, or even only burglary. But if he did not contest his statement the jury would believe it was true. The danger was that although not evidence in law against the others Molloy's confession was almost certain to influence the jury's attitude about them.

The jury retired at 3 p.m. on 8 November and returned the following afternoon with a unanimous verdict. Jimmy Robinson, Michael Hickey and Vincent Hickey were guilty of murder; Pat Molloy was guilty of manslaughter. All four were guilty of aggravated burglary at Yew Tree Farm.

On 12 November Robinson and Vincent Hickey were sentenced to life imprisonment, with a minimum recommendation that they serve 25 years. Michael Hickey, because he was under 18 at the time of the offence, was detained at Her Majesty's Pleasure, and Molloy received 12 years' imprisonment.

NEXT ISSUE:

Bertie Manton
The Luton Sack Murder

Another suspect?

PAUL FOOT

Wh

IT was a senseless, savage crime—the murder of an innocent newsboy who stumbled on a farmhouse robbery and was shot because he knew too much. Four men were jailed over the killing of 13-year-old Carl Bridgewater eight years ago. One died in prison. The others continue to protest their innocence. The Daily Mirror's Paul Foot has carried out a searching inquiry into the case. His conclusion: The wrong men were convicted. In a new book, Murder at the Farm, Foot raises disturbing questions about the police investigation, challenges crucial evidence and points the finger at the man he regards as the prime suspect. "A monstrous injustice has been done," says Foot. "It is high time to put it right."

CARL BRIDGEWATER had just three newspapers left to deliver and his yellow bike almost sailed down the hill towards Yew Tree Farm.

His round took him into the pleasant countryside outside his small West Midlands hometown of Wordsley. This was the best part of the run. Soon he would be heading home...

An hour later, shortly after 5pm, Dr Angus Macdonald drove down the same road on his way home from Wordsley Hospital and decided on impulse to call at the farm.

He often popped in to see the couple who lived there — retired tenant farmer Fred Jones and his cousin Mary Poole. This time he sensed something strange.

Seconds later Dr Macdonald knew he was right. Years later he told me: "Fred and Mary were always talking about burglars, and now they'd come."

Crockery had been swept off surfaces and the cupboards ransacked. But something far more horrible than burglary had happened.

On the settee in the middle of the room lay the body of the newspaper boy.

His feet were on the ground and his head rested on a bolster. His bag, with only two papers in it, ...

a pale blue car — "I am certain a Vauxhall Viva" — turning into the drive-way at about 2.50p...

CARL: Murdered to keep the secrets of Yew Tree Farm

On 14 December 1979, just a month after the four men were convicted of Carl's murder, farmer Hubert Wilkes, who had bought up the land around Yew Tree Farm, hosted a small pre-Christmas drinks party at his home, the neighbouring Holloway House Farm.

His guests were his 34-year-old daughter Jean, his book-keeper Mrs Janet Spencer and Janet's husband Hubert, an ambulance controller at the Corbett Hospital at Stourbridge.

The drinks party at 70-year-old Hubert Wilkes' home had been going well when Spencer excused himself and left the lounge to go to the lavatory. He was gone for a long time. Just after midnight his wife Janet decided to go and check on him. As she went to leave the room via one door, her husband opened another and reappeared. He apologised, saying he was feeling unwell, and vanished again, closing the door behind him.

Moments later Spencer burst back into the room, clutching a sawn-off shotgun. He strode up to the settee where Hubert Wilkes was sitting, pressed the barrels to his best friend's temple, and blew his head off. Janet Spencer tried to wrestle the gun from her husband's grasp.

Jean Wilkes, who had been in another part of the house when the shot was fired, ran into the room and screamed at the sight of the carnage. Bert Spencer punched her in the face with all his force, knocking her to the ground. With her mouth and nose streaming with blood, she managed to scramble through a back door with Spencer, gun in hand, in hot pursuit.

As Jean fled, stumbling across the darkened fields, Spencer loosed off a second shot, which narrowly missed her. After clambering through brambles and a hedge, she hammered on the door of a cottage to raise the alarm.

Back at Holloway House, Janet Spencer was being terrorised by her husband. As she tried to escape via the front door he attacked her, hitting her across the head and body with another gun taken from Hubert Wilkes' gun cabinet.

Seriously wounded

Janet was seriously injured but managed to get into the garden, where she frantically scrambled through a hedge and out onto the road. Mrs Spencer saw an ambulance and flagged it down. It was the one answering the 999 call made from the nearby cottage by the murdered farmer's daughter, Jean.

The ambulance driver, Barrie Thomas, tried to calm the hysterical woman, and as he did so he saw a white Cortina estate car driving slowly up the road towards them. Despite Mrs Spencer's petrified warnings that they would be shot, Thomas bravely approached the car, which stopped. When he looked through the window he was astonished to see his boss, ambulance controller Bert Spencer.

There was a shotgun on the seat next to him. "I am afraid I have had a blackout," he told the astonished Thomas: "I've just shot a friend of mine."

Spencer's trial for the shooting of Hubert Wilkes began at Stafford Crown Court on 23 June. He pleaded not guilty to murder, his defence being that his mind had gone blank, perhaps because he had had too much to drink. He said that although he did not deny the shooting he had not intended to kill his friend.

The jury were not convinced. On 26 June they returned a unanimous verdict of guilty and Spencer was jailed for life.

Left: Hubert Spencer was an ambulance supervisor who was convicted of the senseless shotgun slaying of his friend Hubert Wilkes. The crime took place at Holloway House Farm, just down the road from Yew Tree Farm, only a month after the Bridgewater Four were convicted.

Coincidence?

Apart from the cold-blooded murder of farmer Hubert Wilkes, with many almost identical features to the Carl Bridgewater killing, there were several other reasons to suspect Bert Spencer.

- Spencer drove a blue Vauxhall Viva. Early in the enquiry a witness told police he had seen such a vehicle driving into the lane beside Yew Tree Farm about an hour and a half before the murder.

Hubert Wilkes, who lived here at Holloway House, also worked some of the land belonging to Yew Tree Farm. His murderer, Hubert Spencer, was familiar with both farms, even though he claimed he had never been to Yew Tree Farm when he was first questioned after the murder.

orting THE LONG FIGHT FOR JUSTICE

DAILY MIRROR, Wednesday, September 3, 1986 PAGE 15

killed Carl?

THESE THREE WERE LOCKED UP FOR HIS MURDER, BUT ALL THE SIGNS POINT TO THEIR INNOCENCE

JAILED: Michael Hickey. LIFER: Jimmy Robinson. LIFER: Vincent Hickey.

'I shopped my mates for revenge'

WHEN the murder trial began, all four accused had high hopes of acquittal. The prosecution case was threadbare, unsupported by scientific evidence and put together almost entirely by interrogating police officers, informers and criminals who stood to gain from what they said.

But the shadow of Pat Molloy haunted the case at Stafford Crown Court. And the Irishman's "confession" to being at Yew Tree Farm when Carl was killed was to loom large in the conviction of the other three.

Molloy had told the police he went to the ... with Jimmy Robins... cousins,

MOLLOY: He accused the police

were given life sentences with a recommendation that they each serve at least 25 years.

Michael Hickey, 17, was ordered to be detained indefinitely.

Serving his time, the affair gnawed away at Molloy's conscience. He blasted off letters attacking the judge, lawyers — especially his own — and police and prison officers. H... apologised to Mi... Hickey and also ... up with Robins...

salt, and I was refused a drink.

"During the night I thought long how Vin... was involving me Jim in a murder I ... nothing about.

After 15 years the campaign to free Vincent and Michael Hickey and Jimmy Robinson continues. Here, in June 1993, relatives of the convicted men protest outside the Home Office, calling for the Court of Appeal to review the case for the second time.

Above: Although Hubert Spencer has always denied killing Carl Bridgewater, the case against him is just as good as that against the Bridgewater Four, and casts serious doubt on their convictions. Even if they are eventually released, however, it will do no good for Pat Molloy: he died in prison in 1981.

- Spencer was an ambulance supervisor. According to the witness, the driver of the Vauxhall was dressed in uniform with pips on the shoulders. The police searched records of all organisations whose staff wore uniforms, looking for a man who owned a blue Viva. They came up with Bert Spencer. Coincidentally, Spencer's name had already been mentioned as a suspect in an anonymous phone call to the incident room.
- When Spencer was asked if he was interested in antiques, he said he collected them but was not a dealer. He could help the detectives no further. Weeks later the police discovered Spencer had lied. He was involved in the antique trade and had previously run a small shop in Wordsley.

Enquiries showed that the ambulanceman was a regular visitor to Yew Tree Farm. He had worked on the land many times for farmer Hubert Wilkes. Spencer was also a shooting enthusiast and had often borrowed farmer Wilkes' guns to go rabbit and pigeon shooting on the land. He had visited Yew Tree cottage several times because he was interested in buying a shotgun he heard was for sale. He had been invited in and looked at Fred Jones' antiques. His address and telephone number were even listed in Mr Jones' address book.

Spencer knew Carl

Spencer had made another omission when talking to the detectives. He had failed to say that he knew Carl Bridgewater personally. For five years, between 1970 and 1975, the ambulanceman had lived at 21 Ascot Gardens, Wordsley; the Bridgewater family lived two doors away at No. 25.

After Bert Spencer was arrested for shooting Hubert Wilkes he was interviewed by Detective Chief Superintendent Robert Stewart and Detective Chief Inspector Weslea Watson. The detectives wanted to find out if this second bizarre killing was connected to the Bridgewater case.

In the following days police made more checks to see if Bert Spencer could be Carl's killer, and found another worrying discrepancy.

Detective Sergeant Tony Holdway took away all the daily record sheets for the ambulance liaison office, which should have listed the movements of all employees. Spencer was in charge of the book at the Corbett Hospital and was supposed to log his own movements in it.

Holdway found that the records from January to October 1979 were not there. The detective went to Spencer's regional boss, Barry Chambers. He explained that Spencer's job meant he had to travel between various ambulance stations in the district. It was a strict rule that Spencer had to report all his movements to his area control, which were noted in a log at their Smethwick HQ.

Holdway asked to see the book covering September 1979. When Mr Chambers went to get the book he found it was missing. The book was never found, nor were the missing records from Corbett Hospital.

No motive for the killing of Hubert Wilkes was ever established. The Carl Bridgewater case and the fact that Spencer had been questioned as a suspect only received scant reference during his trial.

Who did kill Carl?

Following the conviction of Hubert Spencer, Ann Whelan and Paul Foot, via his *Daily Mirror* column, mounted a vociferous campaign for the Carl Bridgewater case to be reinvestigated and the Hickeys, Robinson and Molloy to be released.

But on 12 June 1981 they suffered a blow when Pat Molloy collapsed and died while playing football with other inmates in the exercise yard of Walton jail in Liverpool. The campaign to clear the name of the other three continued. In February 1983, Michael and Vincent Hickey made a rooftop protest at Long Lartin jail. Despite freezing conditions, they stayed on the roof for 22 days, until 20 March.

Prison protest

It was not the last protest. On 24 November 1983 Michael Hickey got onto the roof at Gartree Prison. He stayed there, often in sub-zero temperatures, for 89 days until 21 February. It was the longest rooftop protest in British prison history and attracted worldwide publicity and attention.

In March 1987 a documentary programme on the case, titled *Murder at the Farm,* was broadcast by ITV. And in October Home Secretary Douglas Hurd granted the Hickeys and Robinson leave to take their case to the Court of Appeal.

The appeal hearing started in November 1988 and went on until January 1989, before the Lord Chief Justice, Lord Lane. Five days of the appeal were devoted to the evidence against Hubert Spencer. But on 17 March Lord Lane announced that the appeal had been dismissed.

To date Vincent and Michael Hickey and Jimmy Robinson remain in jail, and the campaign by Ann Whelan and Paul Foot continues. Bert Spencer is also still in jail, and has consistently rejected all allegations that he is the killer of Carl Bridgewater.

Bruises: BLACK & BLUE

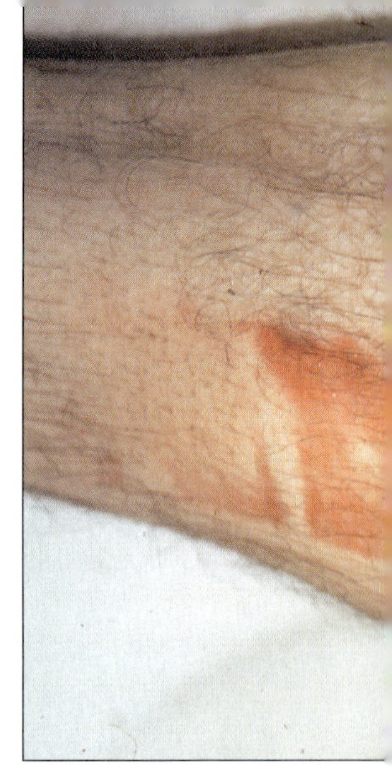

Below: These are the characteristic double bruises caused by caning. Wounds like this, inflicted on a living victim, can be difficult to use in evidence, since the healing process will soon obscure any clues.

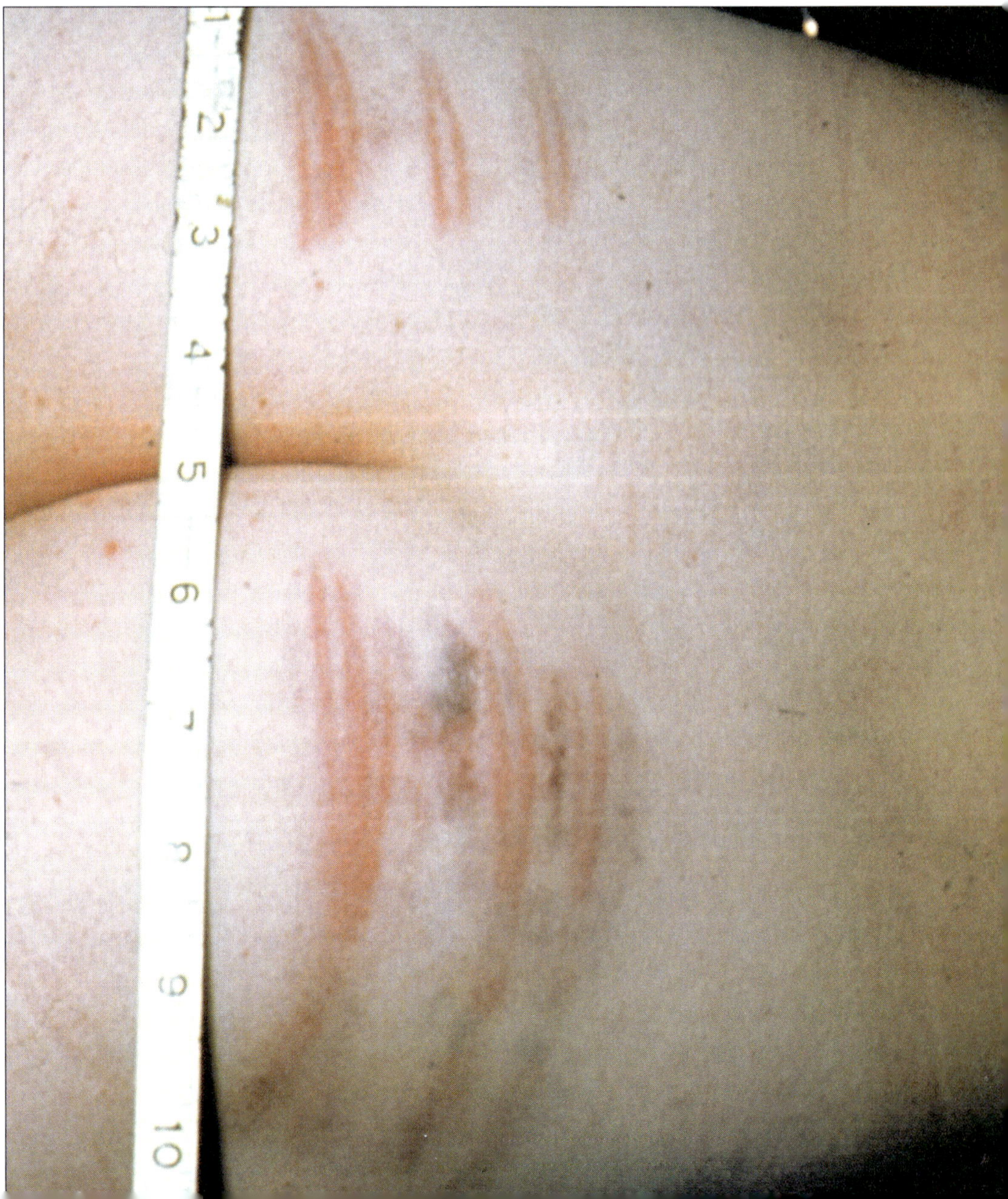

Bruises are the most common form of injury. They can be created by the gentlest of touches, or by a brutal beating. Whatever their origin, they are key pieces of evidence to the forensic investigator.

At first, it might appear that little could be of greater significance to the forensic pathologist than bruises: one might assume that a bruise would inevitably reveal the point of injury, the force exerted, even the shape of the object that caused the injury. But it is not as simple as that.

Burst blood vessels

A bruise, or contusion, is an escape of blood into the tissues due to the rupture of small blood vessels, usually the minor veins or capillaries. A bruise, therefore, can only be inflicted on a living person, since blood will not flow from the vessels after death. Considerable violence inflicted on a corpse may produce injuries that resemble bruising, but these will be relatively small in comparison with the force used. Careful examination during an

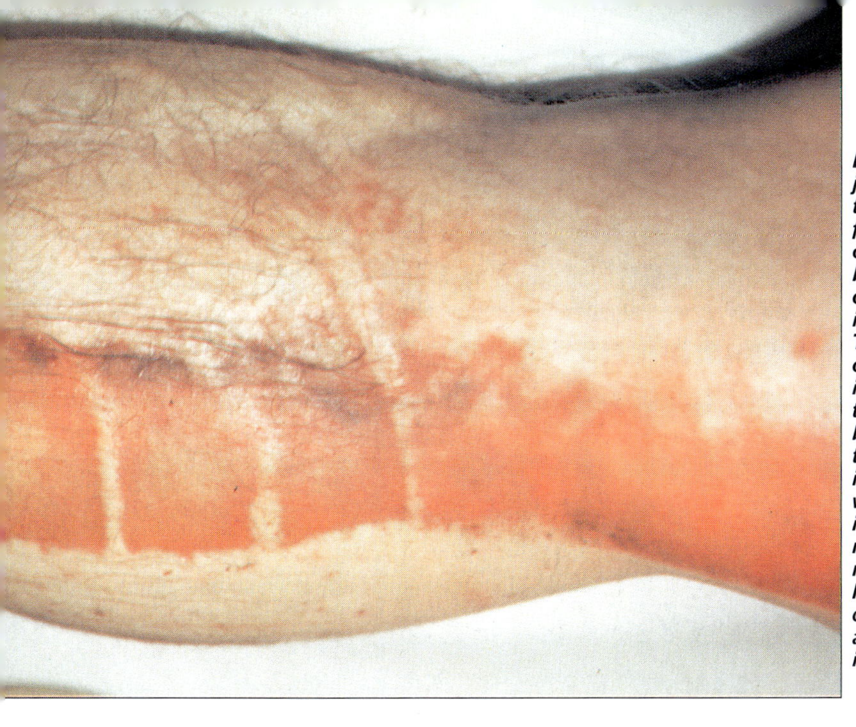

Left: Bruises inflicted just before or at the time of death differ from those which occur on a living body, and can often be of crucial importance in an investigation. The leg of this victim of a hit-and-run incident clearly shows the sharply-defined bruises caused by the tyres of the car involved. Because the victim died in the incident, the body's natural healing mechanism did not have a chance to change the appearance of the injury.

autopsy will reveal that the injury is different from a true bruise.

Although bruises may be associated with a death, the bruise itself is not the cause. They can help to indicate the circumstances of death or an injury and, in certain instances, they may suggest the object that produced a fatal injury. It is in cases of rape, or other forms of criminal assault, however, that bruises, where they occur and the form they take, provide the most telling evidence.

The rupture of the blood vessels and the consequent bruising is usually due to the pressure between the object causing the injury and the underlying bones, and so must be distinguished from abrasions or lacerations. Although the leaking of blood often occurs in quite a shallow area under the skin, the fact that the underlying bone resists the blow with an equal pressure means that deep bruising can occur in any tissue or organ.

Bruises spread

The blood usually spreads through the tissues in a diffuse way, following the fascial planes (the layers of tissue under the skin or between the muscles), and so it seldom reveals the shape or the cause of the bruise. An exception to this is 'intradermal bruising', which occurs only in the uppermost layer of tissue under the skin, and can reproduce the pattern of the injuring object; this is often seen when the skin has been squeezed into grooves, such as the tread of a car tyre or when the victim has been struck with a patterned object such as a plaited whip or a decorative belt.

Beating with a smooth rod often produces 'tramline' bruising: two parallel lines caused by the sides of the rod, rather than by the direct blow. The blood vessels under the point of impact are squeezed and emptied of blood, while those on each side are ruptured.

One interesting case of patterned bruising concerned a miner who was killed in an accident at the coal face. His trunk was covered by parallel zigzag bruises. At first it was thought that these had been caused by the belt of the coal-conveyor that had crushed him to the ground, but the weave of the belt had a very different pattern. It was the technician at Leeds City Mortuary who solved the problem. He pointed out that the bruises matched the weave pattern of the knitted pullover which the dead man had been wearing.

Bruising in living flesh

Generally, bruises are round or oval in shape, and range from a few millimetres to many centimetres across. They are raised above the surface, and this is one of the characteristics that distinguishes them from the apparent bruises caused after death.

If the victim lives, even for only a short time after the blow, the blood will continue to escape into the tissues and the size of the bruise is likely to be larger than

Diamond-shaped bruises on the skin of Margery Gardner indicate where she had been lashed by a whip wielded by sadistic sex-killer Neville Heath. Heath was hanged in 1946 for her murder and the murder of another woman.

A different kind of bruising

There is one type of bruise in which the rupture of the blood vessels is caused, not by pressure, but by suction. This is the 'love bite', which may be found on the neck, breasts or other parts of the body in cases of sexual assault.

What is a bruise?

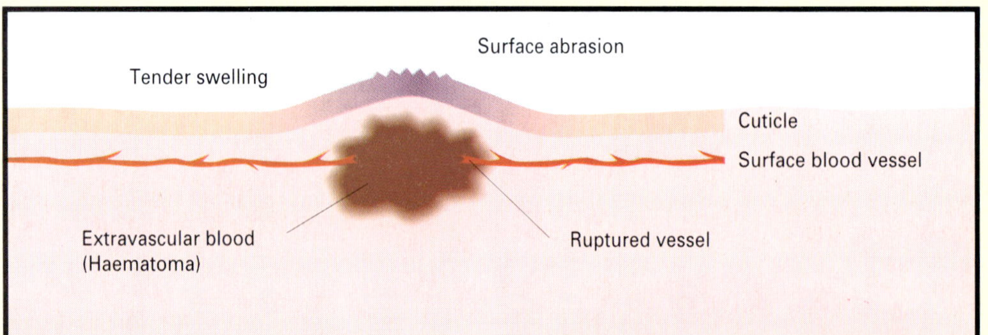

Normal bruises (above) are simply external evidence of internal bleeding. They are usually caused by a blow which ruptures blood vessels but not the skin. Blood leaks out into the surrounding tissue, causing the characteristic darkening of the bruise as well as swelling of the skin.

But bruises do not necessarily appear at the point of impact which caused them. The tramlines characteristic of caning (below) are caused by the blow forcing the blood out of the flesh immediately below the point of impact. The blood gathers on each side, where it causes two long parallel bruises.

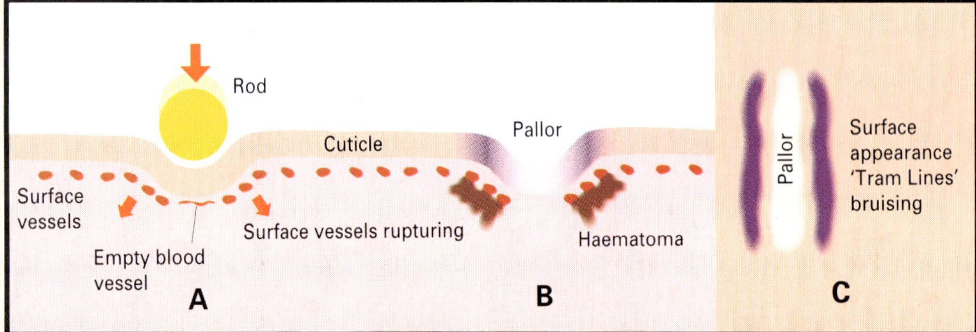

the surface area of the object that caused it. If a large amount of blood escapes, this will continue to diffuse after death. Depending upon the position of the body, it can move considerable distances, both in the dead and the living. The blood may travel towards the surface of the skin – with the familiar effect of a bruise 'coming out' – or through the lower tissues: a bruise on the thigh may subsequently appear at the knee, or an injury high on the scalp may reveal itself as a black eye.

This yellowing bruise is about four days old. Unfortunately, bruises are hard to date with any great accuracy since even on the same person they may heal at greatly differing rates.

Changing colour

With the passage of time a bruise changes colour, due to the breakdown of the haemoglobin in the blood: from red it rapidly changes to blue-black, and then to brown, green, yellow, and it finally fades. But it is impossible to date a bruise with any accuracy, since even two bruises in the same individual may change colour at different rates. In general, a bruise will take between one and two weeks to go through its spectrum of colour changes, although in a fit person some may fade within three or four days.

A number of different coloured bruises on one body is particularly important in cases of alleged child abuse. Parents usually claim that all the bruises are the result of a single accident, but if a bruise is brown/yellow it cannot have been sustained within the previous 24 hours.

Bruises show up most clearly over prominent parts of the body, but the pathologist has to pay particular attention to other areas. In cases of throttling, surface bruises caused by fingers on the neck may be faint and small, although sometimes they are much larger than the pads of the fingers of the assailant. Bruises must also be looked for deep in the neck muscles, as they may not be visible externally.

When the tissues around the shoulder blades show bruising, it often indicates that the body was pushed against the ground or some other surface, such as when the assailant knelt on his victim while throttling him. Bruises on the arms show that the victim was being forcibly restrained. In cases of rape there will usually be bruising of the inner thighs, and sometimes of the genitals, together with bruising of the face and arms as evidence of a struggle.

During autopsy, bruises are looked for in any area where it is suspected they might occur: in the neck in cases of strangulation, and in the inner thighs and genitals in cases of rape. Incision of the area will reveal the characteristic discoloration and tissue damage of bruising, which can be distinguished from post-mortem hypostasis or injuries caused by the dead body being struck or dropped.

There is also likely to be a concentration of white blood cells (leucocytes) in the area, and a section will be taken for microscopic examination. It has been claimed that another type of blood cell, the phagocytes, will

Below: This is the hut in which unsuccessful chicken farmer Norman Thorne's fiancée, Elsie Cameron, died. Thorne admitted disposing of her body. But was Elsie murdered or had she committed suicide?

begin to form a decomposition product of haemoglobin called haemosiderin after 24 hours. This can be detected, but it can also be present as the result of a previous injury, so care must be taken.

Tender flesh bruises easily

Although it is true, in principle, that a heavy blow will produce a larger bruise than a light one, it is difficult to determine the violence of the blow from the appearance of the bruising. Large superficial bruises of tissues such as the eyelids and the external genitals can be caused by only mild violence, whereas tissues close to the bone, as on the scalp, will only bruise with a blow of considerable force.

The very young and the old, the fat and those in poor physical condition also bruise more readily. Even a playful squeeze of a plump, healthy, female arm can produce a bruise that looks like the result of forceful restraint. On the other hand, substantial violence may leave no trace of bruising. Sir Bernard Spilsbury wrote that this occurred in as many as 50 per cent of severe abdominal internal injuries, where the blow caused rupture of a vital organ without rupturing the blood vessels at the point of impact.

And if the pressure has been maintained until after the victim is dead – for instance, if an assailant continues his throttling, or if a car wheel remains in contact with the body – there may also be no bruising.

When Sidney Fox, it is believed, killed his mother and set fire to her room in the Hotel Metropole, Margate, on 22 October 1929, the verdict at the inquest was accidental death.

It was only 11 days later that the body was exhumed, and Sir Bernard Spilsbury announced that Mrs Fox had been strangled. There were no external signs of bruising, nor were the thyroid cartilage or the hyoid bone damaged. Spilsbury said that he had found three internal bruises, one on the tongue, one at the back of the larynx and a third on the thyroid gland.

Sir Sidney Smith was asked to appear for the defence. Smith examined Mrs Fox's larynx in Spilsbury's presence. "'I can't see any sign of a bruise, Spilsbury' I said at length. 'No' agreed Spilsbury. 'You can't see it now. But it was there when I exhumed the body… It became obscure before I put the larynx in formalin. That's why I didn't take a section.'"

Difference of opinion

In court Smith maintained that there was no bruising of the larynx, but due to Spilsbury's reputation the jury found Sidney Fox guilty. Before the sentence was passed, Fox whispered: "My lord, I did not murder my mother. I am innocent." "I believe he was," wrote Smith.

Bruises, therefore, as a number of notorious court cases have shown, cannot be relied upon as an indication of the cause of death, or even that violence has occurred. But they are valuable circumstantial evidence if it is possible to establish their cause.

NEXT ISSUE:

Coroner to the Stars

Elsie Cameron tried to blackmail Thorne into the marriage he had promised by claiming she was pregnant. But she did not get the wedding she wanted.

Bruises convict a murderer

One case in which bruises were crucial in securing a conviction was the death of Elsie Cameron, in which Sir Bernard Spilsbury was called for the prosecution.

Elsie's dismembered body was found buried under the chicken run belonging to her fiancé Norman Thorne on 15 January 1925. Thorne said that he had come home to find her hanging from a beam, and that he had panicked and buried her.

Rope marks on neck?

Much of the argument in court, between Spilsbury and the principal defence witness, Dr Robert Bronte, concerned the question of whether the creases found in the dead girl's neck were natural, or the marks of a rope. But Spilsbury also said that he had found bruises and other injuries "on the head, face, elbow, legs and feet, which together were amply sufficient to account for death from shock, and death which must have occurred very shortly after those injuries were inflicted."

Since it was highly improbable that Elsie Cameron could have injured herself in this way before hanging, the bruises must have been inflicted before death, and had presumably been the cause of death, which conflicted with Thorne's insistence that he had found her already dead. And when it was further pointed out that there were no rope marks on the beam, the jury had no hesitation in finding Thorne guilty of murder.

Below: Elsie's dismembered remains were found buried beneath Thorne's chicken run. Bruises on the body convinced Sir Bernard Spilsbury that she had been beaten to death.

ROB, BURN — AND — KILL

CARL PANZRAM

Thirty-seven-year-old Carl Panzram had just been arrested for burglary when this police photograph was taken. A five-year sentence for the crime would have been normal, but his menacing performance in court, in addition to his long record, meant that he was sentenced to 25 years in the Federal penitentiary at Fort Leavenworth, Kansas.

"If you examine my crimes, you will find that I have consistently followed one idea. I preyed on the weak, the harmless and the unsuspecting. This lesson I was taught by others: might makes right."

Everyone said the new prisoner would be trouble. The warden of the jail where he had been held on remand warned that he was violent and unpredictable, that he would certainly try to escape and would have to be kept in segregation. Although he had been sentenced only for burglary, he had boasted of killing several times, and at least some of his claims seemed to check out.

At his trial he had claimed from the dock that: "My conscience doesn't bother me. I have no conscience. I believe the whole human race should be exterminated. I'll do my best to do it every chance I get." His performance had earned him a sentence of 25 years.

T. B. White, Warden of Leavenworth Penitentiary, was sure his men could handle the newcomer. They were used to troublemakers. There were 3,700 of America's worst criminals locked in the Federal prison in Kansas. This was more than twice as many as it was built to hold, and few prisoners got a cell to themselves.

When Carl Panzram was transferred from Washington District Jail on 30 January 1929, the Deputy Warden, Fred Zerbst, assigned him to the laundry. Panzram, a great bear of a man with a pen-

Carl Panzram joined the US Army briefly when he was 16, but spent most of his service career in the United States Military Penitentiary at Fort Leavenworth, on the plains of Kansas. During that time he was part of the convict labour force from 'Little Top', as the tough prison was called, which was used to build the nearby Federal penitentiary – 'Big Top' – in which he was to serve his last prison term two decades later.

Biography

A life of crime

Carl Panzram was born in East Grand Forks, Minnesota, on 28 June 1891, the last of eight children born to a pair of German dirt-farmers. Panzram's father, a heavy drinker, was often away, and abandoned his family when Carl was about seven. Life was hard. The Panzram children went to school in the day and worked in the fields at night. His brothers left home as soon as they were able, and Carl began to run wild.

When Carl was 11 he stole some food and a pistol from a neighbour's house and hopped on a freight train to go West and become a cowboy. He was caught and sent to the Minnesota State Training School at Red Wing. There, a regimen of work and beatings, Christian indoctrination and sexual abuse hardened Panzram's rebellious tendencies into a deep hatred of authority. Released into his mother's care in January 1906, he soon ran off and began wandering. He was gang-raped by some hoboes in a box-car, then was caught during a burglary and sent to a reform school in Montana.

After that his life was one long round of theft, arson – he never passed up a chance to rob and burn down a church – and lengthening prison sentences under various aliases. Sometimes he served his time, and sometimes he escaped.

Robbing around the world

He fought a one-man war against Oregon State Penitentiary, which ended with his escape in May 1918. He robbed his way across country to New York, where he took out merchant seamen's papers and began to travel the world, stealing and burning as he went.

In the summer of 1920, back in the USA, he made his biggest score, stealing $40,000-worth of bonds and jewellery in a burglary. With the proceeds, he bought a yacht and embarked on his career of murder.

Panzram came from a poor family of German immigrants. But, unlike his siblings, he got into trouble from an early age and was sent to the Minnesota State Training School (right) at the age of 12. Thus began a process of brutalisation which would turn a delinquent into one of the most vicious criminals in history.

Below: Panzram served a brief sentence in Glasgow's Barlinnie Prison, in a criminal career which covered four continents.

etrating glare and huge, restless hands, listened impassively as Zerbst outlined the rules of the prison, then said, flatly: "I'll kill the first man that bothers me."

Leavenworth's laundry, stifling hot in the summer and freezing in winter, was not a soft option. It was run by a civilian, R. G. Warnke, who was a stalwart of the local chapter of the Ku Klux Klan and seemed to enjoy dealing with truculent prisoners.

Panzram settled down to his work. He said little to anyone, and totally ignored his cell mate. He spent his time in his cell reading. He had a taste for philosophy, particularly the work of the Germans, Nietzsche and Schopenhauer. The only letters he got were from Henry Lesser, a guard at the Washington District Jail who had befriended the brooding prisoner.

Panzram punished

New Federal laws against possession of drugs and bootlegging were increasing the prison population, and the quality of the food was falling. Better provisions could be had on the prison black market, and Panzram began to earn a few cents by doing wealthy convicts' extra laundry for cash. Warnke got wind of this, and had Panzram stripped of what few privileges he had and sent to the Hole, a chill punishment cell too small to lie down in.

Contrary to normal prison practice, Panzram was then sent back to the laundry. Silently, he returned to work, but his resentment was building. On 20 June

Above: At the age of 21 Carl Panzram was convicted of burglary in Montana under the name of Jeff Davis. After escaping from Deer Lodge Prison, he was caught a week later after another burglary. He was tried and convicted under the name of Jefferson Rhoades. Unfortunately for Panzram, he was sentenced to the same prison he had broken out of. He was immediately recognised on arrival at Deer Lodge, where his sentence was extended by a year.

Prisoner'

Henry Lesser was working as a guard in the Washington District Jail when Panzram was brought there in August 1928 after his arrest in Baltimore. The idealistic Lesser, just 25, was struck by the prisoner's demeanour and the fact that he said his purpose in life was to "reform people". Later, Panzram confided that the only way to reform people was to kill them.

Tortured and beaten

In October, guards discovered that Panzram was planning an escape. He was tortured and beaten and confessed to – or boasted of – killing three boys. The authorities chose not to believe him, seeing him as a chiseller – someone who confessed to crimes others had committed in order to get extradited to

he was marched to work as usual. He melted away into the back of the laundry, where the remains of some large packing cases, which had once contained washing machines, were strewn about.

About five minutes later, Warnke walked through the laundry and was suddenly confronted by Panzram, who was wielding a 10-lb bar of iron he had wrenched from one of the cases. He felled the supervisor with a blow to the head, then leaned over his quivering body, pounding him with the bar until he was still.

Looking for the deputy warden

Then Panzram set off at a strange, shuffling run – his ankles had been broken in an attempted escape from a previous prison and had set badly because he had received no medical treatment. He was looking for Zerbst who, fortunately for him, was not in his office. Then he went

After being found guilty of burglary in 1928, Panzram was sent to the grim, red brick block of Washington District Jail (above). While he was there, one small act of kindness by guard Henry Lesser (right) affected the violent criminal deeply, and the two men began a wary friendship, which was continued by letter when Panzram was transferred to the Federal penitentiary in Kansas.

Left: Only once before had a correctional official tried to get through to Panzram. Charles A. Murphy of Oregon State Penitentiary was a pioneer prison official who believed that more could be achieved by trusting prisoners than by the regime of extreme brutality then common in American prisons. Panzram had at first responded well to the scheme, but after several months he betrayed Murphy's trust by absconding after getting drunk while on an evening's leave from the prison.

friend

another state.

Lesser felt sorry for Panzram, and gave him a dollar. This was one of the very few acts of kindness Panzram had ever experienced from a prison officer, and it had a deep effect on him. He began to write his life story for Lesser, using materials the guard smuggled in for him, and continued to write to him after his transfer to Leavenworth.

Lesser spent the best part of 40 years trying to get others interested in Panzram's confessions. They were eventually published in 1970 in a book called *Killer*, by Thomas Gaddis and James Long, since hailed as a crime-writing classic.

Lesser and Panzram kept in contact even after the convict's transfer to Leavenworth. Panzram's letters gave one of the first and still one of the best glimpses into the mind of an intelligent psychopath.

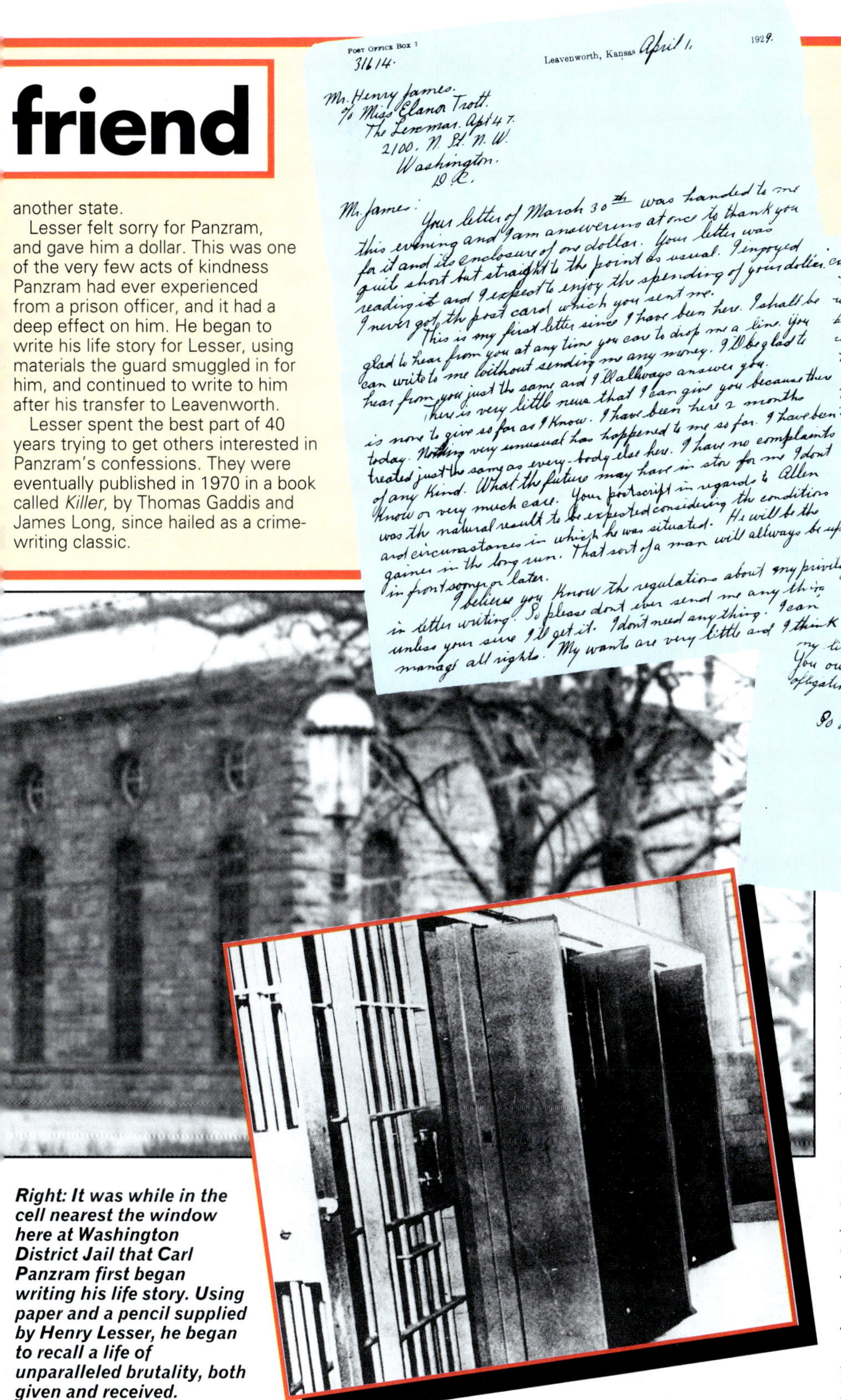

Post Office Box 7
31614.
Leavenworth, Kansas April 1, 1929.

Mr. Henry James.
% Miss Elanor Trott.
The Lenmar. Apt 47.
2100. N. St. N. W.
Washington.
D. C.

Mr. James:
Your letter of March 30th was handed to me
this evening and I am answering at once to thank you
for it and its enclosure of one dollar. Your letter was
quite short but straight to the point as usual. I enjoyed
reading it and I expect to enjoy the spending of your dollar.
I never got the post card which you sent me.
This is my first letter since I have been here. I shall be
glad to hear from you at any time you care to drop me a line. You
can write to me without sending me any money. I'll be glad to
hear from you just the same and I'll allways answer you.
There is very little news that I can give you because there
is none to give so far as I know. I have been here 2 months
today. Nothing very unusual has happened to me so far. I have been
treated just the same as every-body else here. I have no complaints
of any kind. What the future may have in store for me I dont
know or very much care. Your postscript in regards to Allen
was the natural result to be expected considering the conditions
and circumstances in which he was situated. He will be the
gainer in the long run. That sort of a man will allways be up
in front sooner or later.
I believe you know the regulations about my privilege
in letter writing. So please dont ever send me any thing
unless your sure I'll get it. I dont need any thing. I can
manage all rights. My wants are very little and I think

can satisfy them. I have met a number of my old pals
here who knew me years ago. I still have my perpetual
...uch and I dont believe it will ever wear off until I pass out
...bletely. That time cant come too quick to suit me. Just at
...ent I pass my time in sleeping, eating, working, reading
thinking. And the last is not the least.
I have wondered about you a number of times and since
...ing your letter, the thought has occured to me that you may
...ping house or getting ready to. The name sounds English.
...of musical too. I had hopes that you would by
...ime have found yourself in a better job with more
...eat surroundings and a cleaner also. phere. Take
...e and drop that job like you would poison. Thats no
...a job for you. Your built for better things than that.
your literary lady friend and yourself getting along
writing the Biography of the meanest man you ever
I have been passing my time away by scribbling a
and then. So far I have written about 30 or 40
...words. Should you ever come to this place and if
for it I would gladly make you a present of
my little contribution to the worlds worst literature.
You owe me nothing but I consider myself under some
obligation to you.
Well, I'll wind up this tale of woe, by saying
So Long and best wishes.
I am very truly
Carl Panzram #31614.
Box. 7.
Leavenworth.
Kansas.

Right: It was while in the cell nearest the window here at Washington District Jail that Carl Panzram first began writing his life story. Using paper and a pencil supplied by Henry Lesser, he began to recall a life of unparalleled brutality, both given and received.

to the isolation block, demanding to be let in. The guard on duty insisted he put down the bloody bar. Panzram tossed it aside and strolled into an isolation cell.

From this point until his trial, on 15 April 1930, he was treated far more humanely than he had ever been before in a prison. "If, in the beginning I had been treated as well as I am now," he wrote, "then there wouldn't have been so many people in this world that have been robbed, raped and killed."

Panzram killed 22 people, some of them for money, some for sex, and some, apparently, for the pure hell of it. He used a gun for preference, but was prepared to use any weapon that came to hand.

He started his killing career in 1920, when he was flush with the results of a particularly successful robbery.

Murder at sea

After buying and registering a yacht, he took to hanging around the Seamen's Union offices in New York and offering sailors big money to join his crew. When they arrived with their gear he would get them drunk, wait till they were asleep, and kill them with a .45 automatic he had stolen in a burglary. Then, at dead of night, he would row out with the bodies, weight them with rocks, and tip them into the water. Ten men died in this way in the space of about three weeks.

Later, the yacht was wrecked in a storm. Panzram started wandering again, joining a ship for Europe. From there he went to Africa, where he worked for an American oil company in Angola.

Fed to the crocodiles

In Luanda, he kidnapped, raped and killed an 11-year-old black boy. A day or two later he hired a canoe and six men to go hunting in Lobito Bay. He killed all six with a Luger and fed them to the crocodiles. His only motive appeared to be to steal the canoe, which was itself stolen from him from its moorings later that day.

By the summer of 1922 he had made his way back to New York. On 18 July he raped a 12-year-old boy in Salem, Massachusetts, and beat him to death with a rock, then moved on, financing himself with burglary.

He stole a yacht, then repainted it to pass it off as the one he had registered and lost. When a man offered to buy it, then

Panzram's early life was spent in back-breaking work on a farm in Minnesota.

Killer without a conscience

Carl Panzram was one of the most dedicated and unrepentant criminals America ever produced. "In my lifetime," he wrote, "I have murdered 21 human beings, I have committed thousands of burglaries, robberies, larcenies and arsons and last but not least I have committed sodomy on more than 1,000 male human beings. For all these things I am not in the least bit sorry.

"I have done as I was taught to do. I have consistently followed one idea through all my life. I preyed on the weak, the harmless, the unsuspecting. This lesson I was taught by others; might makes right."

Hating the world

Panzram first learned this bitter creed from a harsh and punishing home life, then had it reinforced at Red Wing, where he was sexually abused and beaten by other inmates and by the staff. "I began to hate those who abused me. Then I began to think I would have my revenge just as soon and as often as I could injure someone else. Anyone at all would do. If I couldn't injure those who injured me, then I would injure someone else. I made up my mind that I would rob, burn, destroy and kill everywhere I went and everybody I could for as long as I lived."

He insisted that he was not mad, and certainly wasn't by the legal standard. In fact, he was remarkably clear-thinking, with a disciplined mind.

Panzram killed out of hate and disgust. He despised the weak for being weak and the strong for trying to dominate him. "I don't believe in man, God nor Devil," he declared. "I hate the whole damned race including myself." Tired of his hatred, he eventually courted death for himself. As far as he was concerned, his death sentence was "the first and only time in my life of battling with the law that I ever did get justice from the law." Pausing only to insist that the attendant priests be removed, he rushed to the gallows as if greeting an old friend.

The Minnesota State Training School in Red Wing is where brutality became the norm for Carl Panzram.

pulled a gun on him in an attempt to steal it, Panzram killed him with a .38 pistol he had stolen from a police commissioner's yacht in Connecticut and dumped him over the side.

In August 1923 he murdered another boy, William Berger, in New Haven, strangling him with his own belt. Soon after, he was caught in the act of robbing a railroad baggage room in New York, and sentenced to five years.

He was sent to Clinton Prison for incorrigibles in Dannemora, which practised the harshest regime in the country, with cells just over six feet long and 40 inches wide, and the bars in the door so close together that the inmates could not put their fingers through them.

ISBN 1-85875-015-6
9 781858 750156

He filled his time with plans for escape and fantasies of mass murder once he was out. "My plan," he wrote, "was to rob, rape and kill everybody I could, anybody and everybody." Some of his ideas, like putting arsenic in a town's water supply, were purely for the sake of destruction. Others were to make him a lot of money.

Murderous sabotage schemes

He planned to use a bomb to wreck a passenger train in a tunnel, fill it with poison gas, then put on a gas mask and oxygen tank and steal everything he could carry away. With the proceeds, he planned to make a killing on the stock market by starting a war between Britain and the USA. He worked out detailed plans to sink a British battleship in the Hudson River, or use a British schooner as a floating bomb to destroy the Panama Canal.

After his release, he was free for less than six weeks, time enough to carry out about a dozen burglaries and kill another youth, a newsboy called Alex Luszzock. Then a young fence, Joe Czerivinski, was caught pawning a stolen radio in Baltimore and told the police where he had got it. The Baltimore police arrested Panzram, who for once told them his correct age and name and gave his occupation as "thief".

After killing Warden Warnke, Panzram was declared insane by a Sanity Commission, but this did not prevent him being convicted of murder and sentenced to death. He was satisfied with the verdict, and instructed his court-appointed attorney not to appeal.

Various groups opposed to capital punishment immediately began working on his behalf, hoping to get his sentence commuted to one of life imprisonment in solitary confinement. Panzram resisted vigorously, sending the main group a long letter outlining what he felt was the justice of the sentence and telling them that he wished they all had one neck and that he had his hands on it. "I would sure put you out of your misery," he concluded, "just the same as I have done with numbers of other people."The hangman put Carl Panzram out of his misery on 5 September 1930.